# Asian Adventures

# A - Z!

Written by Yobe Qiu

Illustrated by Jade Le

# Aa

A is for Asia, the continent.

A is for Agra,

the city of the Taj Mahal.

A is also for beautiful áo dài dresses...

worn by Vietnamese women.

# Bb

B is for Bangkok.

# B is for Bhutan.

B is also for bibimbap,
rice served in hot stone bowls in Korea.

# Cc

C is for Cambodia.

# C is for China.

C is also for saucy
and spicy chow mein.

# Dd

D is for Delhi, the capital of India.

D is for delicious dim sum.

D is also for durians,
Asia's smelliest fruit loved by many.

# Ee

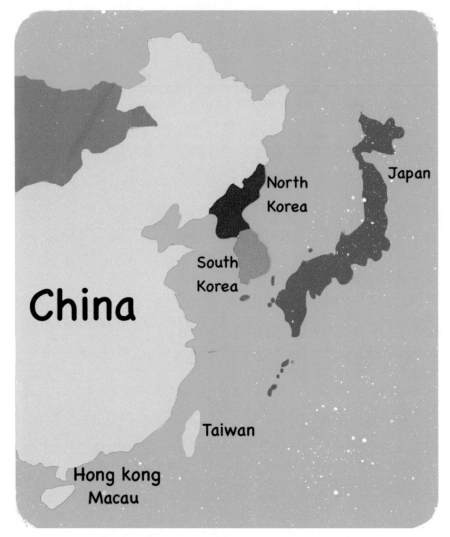

E is for East Asia,
home to some of the busiest Asian cities.

E is for elephants, treasured and respected animals in many Asia cultures.

E is also for egg rolls.

# Ff

F is for Fuji, Japan.

F is for Forbidden City, where many of the emperors and their families lived in Beijing.

F is also for the exciting
full moon parties in Thailand.

# Gg

G is for the Great Wall of China.

G is for gamelan,
a traditional music form from Indonesia.

G is also for Ginger, used in food and tea.

# Hh

H is for the Himalayas.

H is for Holi, a festival of colors in India.

H is also for Hong Kong, home of
the most diverse and delicious food!

# Ii

I is for India.

I is for Indonesia.

I is also for the very famous Ice and Snow festival in China.

# Jj

J is for Jakarta, Indonesia.

# J is for Jeju, South Korea.

J is also for the tropical jackfruits found in Malaysia.

# Kk

K is for Kuala Lumpur,
the largest city in Malaysia.

K is for Khmer, the people and national language of Cambodia.

K is also for Komodo dragons, the world's largest lizards, found in Indonesia.

# Ll

L is for Laos.

L is for Lhasa, Tibet.

L is also for leche flan, a sweet
caramel custard served in the Philippines.

# Mm

M is for Malaysia.

# M is for Macau and Mongolia.

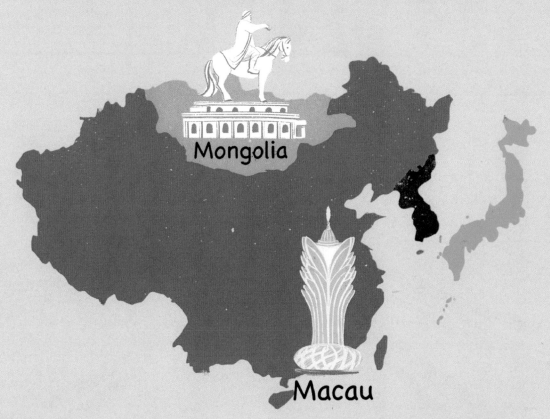

Mongolia

Macau

M is also for sweet
and spicy flavored
mace spice in Indonesia.

# Nn

N is for Nepal.

# N is for North Korea.

# N is also for noodle soups enjoyed by many.

# Oo

O is for Osaka,
a city in Japan with a real castle!

O is for Orussey Market,
a popular traditional market in Cambodia.

O is also for Oyster sauce
used to cook many delicious Asian entrées.

# Pp

P is for Philippines.

P is for the many different variations of papaya salad.

P is also for pho, warm Vietnamese soup noodles.

# Qq

Q is for Qutub Minar, the tallest minaret in the world built of bricks in India.

Q is for Qipao,
a traditional Chinese dress.

Q is also for queso, Filipino cheese ice cream.

# Rr

R is for rickshaw.

R is for rice.

R is also for the very tasty roti bread.

# Ss

S is for Singapore.

S is for Seoul.

S is also for saké and colorful sushi.

# Tt

T is for Thailand.

T is for Tibet.

T is also for tea ceremonies
enjoyed by many in Taiwan.

# Uu

U is for Ulaanbaatar,
the capital of Mongolia.

U is for Ube.
Sweet Filipino dessert
made out of mashed purple yams.

U is also for udon noodles.

# Vv

V is for Vietnam.

V is for Vientiane, largest city of Laos.

V is also for vermicelli.

# Ww

W is for Wuhan, China.

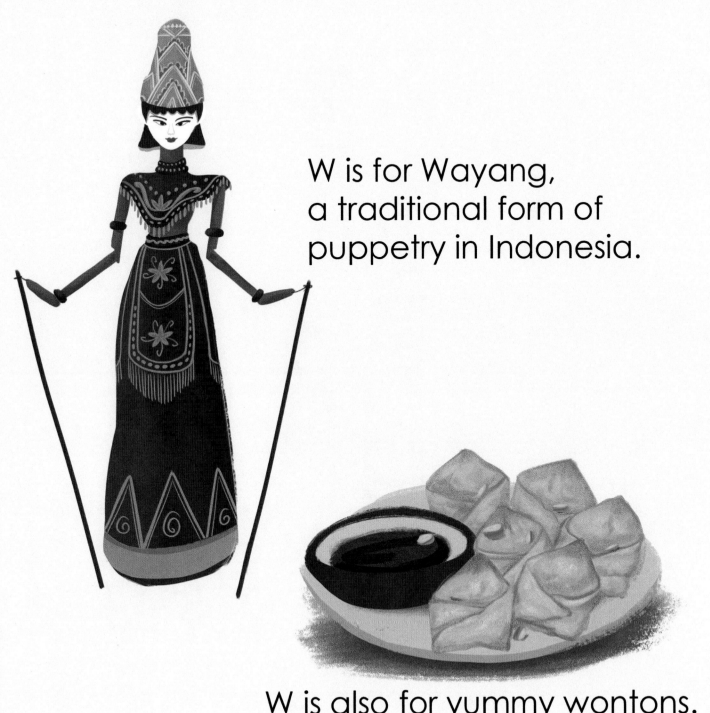

W is for Wayang,
a traditional form of
puppetry in Indonesia.

W is also for yummy wontons.

# Xx

X is for Xiamen, a city in China.

X is for xie xie, which means thank you in Chinese.

X is also for xiao long bao, delicious soup dumplings from Shanghai.

# Yy

Y is for Yin and Yang.

Y is for Yen, the Japanese currency.

Y is also for yang chow fried rice.

# Zz

Z is for Zen Gardens.

Rat Ox Tiger Rabbit

Dragon Snake Horse Goat

Monkey Rooster Dog Pig

Z is for the zodiac.

Z is also for zongzi,
eaten during the Dragon Boat Festival.

**Author**

Yobe Qiu is an educator, entrepreneur, mom, and bestselling author with a passion for storytelling. As an educator, Yobe taught children and their families to embrace love and diverse cultures. When she identified a need for more multicultural books, she decided to create her own children's stories featuring Asian characters and cultures. Today, Yobe is proud to publish books that help children like her daughter feel seen, heard, and represented. Yobe looks forward to writing many more stories in the years to come.

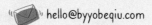 hello@byyobeqiu.com    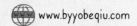 www.byyobeqiu.com

Jade is a Vietnamese artist who works as a full-time freelance illustrator in Singapore. Her love for drawing began as a hobby and gradually evolved into a blooming career. One of her greatest joys is assisting inspired authors to present their engaging stories in beautiful artworks. When she has free time, Jade draws inspiration from everyday life. She hopes you will enjoy her work as much as she has fun illustrating it.

 jadele.illustration@gmail.com    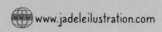 www.jadeleiIustration.com

**Illustrator**

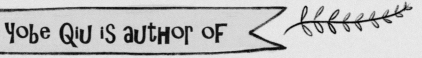

## Yobe Qiu is author of

> » Our Lunar New Year
>
> » Our Moon Festival
>
> » Our Double Fifth Celebration
>
> » The Asian Holidays Children's Activity Book
>
> » Asian Adventures A-Z

If you enjoyed this book, or any of Yobe Qiu's books, please leave a review. Your kindness and support are greatly appreciated!

Published in New York, NY by By Yobe Qiu Publishing

www.ByYobeQiu.com

ISBN: 978-1-7355835-4-9

Book cover design & illustrations by Jade Le.

Made in the USA
Las Vegas, NV
23 August 2023

76523781R00033